Merrily Comes Our Harvest In

Poems for Thanksgiving

selected by
Lee Bennett Hopkins
Illustrations by
Ben Shecter

WORDSONG
BOYDS MILLS PRESS

Published by Wordsong
Boyds Mills Press, Inc.
A Highlights Company
910 Church Street
Honesdale, Pennsylvania 18431

Printed in Mexico
Publisher Cataloging-in-Publication Data
Main entry under title.
  Merrily comes our harvest in : poems for Thanksgiving / poems selected by Lee Bennett
Hopkins ; illustrations by Ben Shecter.
[32]p. : ill. ; cm.
Includes index.
Originally published by Harcourt Brace Jovanovich, New York, in 1978.
Summary : A collection of twenty poems about Thanksgiving.
ISBN 1-878093-57-6
1. Thanksgiving Day—Juvenile poetry. 2. Children's poetry, American. [1.Thanksgiving
Day—Poetry. 2. American poetry—Collections.]
I. Shecter, Ben, ill. II. Title.
811 / .008—dc20   1993
Library of Congress Catalog Card Number: 91-70411

The text of this book is set in 11-point Galliard.
The illustrations are line drawings.
Distributed by St. Martin's Press

10 9 8 7 6 5 4 3 2 1

Every effort has been made to trace the ownership of all copyrighted material and to secure
the necessary permissions to reprint these selections. In the event of any question arising as
to the use of any material, the editor and the publisher, while expressing regret for any
inadvertent error, will be happy to make the necessary correction in future printings.

"The Little Girl and the Turkey" from ALL TOGETHER NOW by Dorothy Aldis. Copyright
© 1925, 1926, 1927, 1928, 1934, 1939, 1952 by Dorothy Aldis; copyright renewed.
Reprinted with permission of G.P. Putnam's Sons.

"Thanksgiving Magic" by Rowena Bastin Bennett originally appeared in CHILD LIFE
MAGAZINE. Reprinted with permission of Kenneth C. Bennett.

This one's for
Anna Bier
who makes lives merry!

HARVEST

The boughs do shake and the bells do ring,
So merrily comes our harvest in,
Our harvest in, our harvest in,
So merrily comes our harvest in.

We've ploughed, we've sowed,
We've reaped, we've mowed,
We've got our harvest in.

Anonymous

I LIKE FALL

I like fall:
it always smells smoky,
chimneys wake early,
the sun is poky;

Folks go past
in a hustle and bustle,
and when I scuff
in the leaves, they rustle.

I like fall:
all the hills are hazy,
and after a frost
the puddles look glazy;

And nuts rattle down
where nobody's living,
and pretty soon . . .
it will be THANKSGIVING.

Aileen Fisher

NOVEMBER'S GIFT

November is a lady
  In a plain gray coat
That's very closely buttoned
  Up around her throat.

And after she's been roaming
  All around the town,
She reaches in her pocket,
  Deep, deep down,

Then pulls out a present,
  And with laughter gay,
Says to everybody,
  "Here's Thanksgiving Day!"

Alice Crowell Hoffman

FIRST THANKSGIVING

Three days we had,
   feasting, praying, singing.

Three days outdoors at wooden tables,
Colonists and Indians together,
Celebrating a full harvest,
A golden summer of corn.

   We hunted the woods, finding
   Venison, deer, and wild turkey.

   We brought our plump geese and ducks,
   Great catches of silver fish.

   We baked corn meal bread with nuts,
   Journey cake, and steaming succotash.

   We roasted the meat on spits
   Before huge, leaping fires.

   We stewed our tawny pumpkins
   In buckets of bubbling maple sap.

Three days we had,
   feasting, praying, singing.

Three days outdoors at wooden tables,
Colonists and Indians together,
Celebrating a full harvest,
Praying, each to our God.

Myra Cohn Livingston

FIRST THANKSGIVING

If I had been a Pilgrim child
Among the fields and forests wild
Where deer and turkey used to roam,
A cabin would have been my home
With fireplace and earthen floor
And bearskins hanging at the door.
I would have gathered berries bright
For candles fragrantly alight.
And dug for clams and picked the corn
And laid the table smooth and worn.
Or hunted nuts hard-shelled and good
And helped in any way I could,
With time to laugh and play and run
When Indian children came for fun.
And on the first Thanksgiving Day
I would have met with friends to pray
And thank the Lord for all his care
In keeping us together there.

Margaret Hillert

13

THANKSGIVING TIME

When all the leaves are off the boughs,
    And nuts and apples gathered in,
And cornstalks waiting for the cows,
    And pumpkins safe in barn and bin;

Then Mother says: "My children dear,
    The fields are brown, and Autumn flies;
Thanksgiving Day is very near,
    And we must make Thanksgiving pies!"

Anonymous

THE PUMPKIN

You may not believe it, for hardly could I:
I was cutting a pumpkin to put in a pie,
And on it was written in letters most plain
"You may hack me in slices, but I'll grow again."

I seized it and sliced it and made no mistake
As, with dough rounded over, I put it to bake:
But soon in the garden as I chanced to walk,
Why, there was that pumpkin entire on his stalk!

Robert Graves

15

A THANKSGIVING THOUGHT

The day I give thanks for having a nose
Is Thanksgiving Day, for do you suppose
That Thanksgiving dinner would taste as good
If you couldn't smell it? I don't think it would.
Could apple pies baking—turkey that's basting
Not be for smelling? Just be for tasting?
It's a cranberry-cinnamon-onion bouquet!
Be thankful for noses on Thanksgiving Day.

Bobbi Katz

16

THANKSGIVING MAGIC

Thanksgiving Day I like to see
Our cook perform her witchery.
She turns a pumpkin into pie
As easily as you or I
Can wave a hand or wink an eye.
She takes leftover bread and muffin
And changes them to turkey stuffin'.
She changes cranberries to sauce
And meats to stews and stews to broths;
And when she mixes gingerbread
It turns into a man instead
With frosty collar 'round his throat
And raisin buttons down his coat.
Oh, some like magic made by wands,
      And some read magic out of books,
And some like funny spells and charms
      But I like magic made by cooks!

Rowena Bastin Bennett

THANKSGIVING WISHES

I wish you all that pen and ink
      Could write, and then some more!
I hope you cannot even think
      Of half you're thankful for.

I hope your table holds a wealth
      Of prime Thanksgiving fare,
And Love and Peace and Joy and Health
      Will all be seated there.

I trust your guests will all be bright,
      But none of them too wise,
And each will bring an appetite
      For mince or pumpkin pies.

I hope the fowls will all be fat,
      The cider sweet to quaff,
And when you snap a Wishbone, that
      You'll win the larger half!

Arthur Guiterman

APPLE PIE

Apple pie,
pumpkin pie,
turkey on the dish!
We can see
we can eat
everything we
wish, wish, wish, wish.

Grandma's here,
Grandpa's here,
cousins bright and gay.
Aunts and uncles
share with us
this good Thanksgiving
day, day, day, day.

Thank you, God,
thank you, God,
for good things to eat.
Thank you also
for this day
when we with friendly hearts
do meet, meet, meet.

Else Holmelund Minarik

WHAT THE LITTLE GIRL SAID

Oh, for sweet potatoes and peas,
I will pass my plate and say please,
    And tomatoes so red,
    And fresh raisin bread—
Who wouldn't want plenty of these?

And turkey's a special delight.
I could eat it from morning till night.
    The mince pie is great,
    But I'm here to state:
No turnips! Not even one bite.

Lee Blair

TURKEY TIME

You should come to visit us,
To see our way of living;
We have our way of doing things,
Especially on Thanksgiving.

We have:

Turkey soup and turkey legs,
Turkey wings and turkey eggs.
Turkey broth and turkey liver
(My mom can eat all you give her).
Turkey toes and turkey beaks,
Turkey claws and turkey cheeks.
Turkey salad and turkey dressing
(A ton of that, I am guessing).
Turkey sauce and turkey steak,
Turkey pie and turkey cake.
Turkey thighs and turkey knees,
Turkey stew and turkey teas.
Turkey juice and turkey leathers,
Everything, but turkey feathers.

Dean Hughes

23

THE LITTLE GIRL AND THE TURKEY

The little girl said
As she asked for more:
"But what is the Turkey
Thankful for?"

Dorothy Aldis

THANKSGIVING

I feel so stuffed inside my skin
And full of little groans,
I know just how the turkey felt
Before it turned to bones.

Margaret Hillert

THANKSGIVING

I'm glad that I was good today,
   As good as I was able.
I'm glad to be inside this house
   And sitting at this table.

I'm glad that it's Thanksgiving Day
   And all the world is merry,
And I'm glad I have a fork
   And that the pie is cherry.

Marchette Chute

26

DAY IS DONE

We've eaten all our dinner,
prayed our prayers,
wished our wishes.

Now it's time to get to work
and wash up
all these dishes!

Lee Bennett Hopkins

THANKSGIVING

Thank You
    for all my hands can hold—
        apples red
          and melons gold,
            yellow corn
                both ripe and sweet,
                  peas and beans
                     so good to eat!

Thank You
    for all my eyes can see—
        lovely sunlight,
          field and tree,
            white cloud-boats
                in sea-deep sky,
                  soaring bird
                    and butterfly.

Thank You
    for all my ears can hear—
        birds' song echoing
          far and near,
            songs of little
                stream, big sea,
                  cricket, bullfrog,
                    duck and bee!

Ivy O. Eastwick

THANKSGIVING DAY

Brave and high-souled Pilgrims, you who knew no fears,
How your words of thankfulness go ringing down the years;
May we follow after; like you, work and pray,
And with hearts of thankfulness keep Thanksgiving Day.

Annette Wynne

ALL IN A WORD

T for time to be together,
  turkey, talk, and tangy weather.

H for harvest stored away,
  home, and hearth, and holiday.

A for autumn's frosty art,
  and abundance in the heart.

N for neighbors, and November,
  nice things, new things to remember.

K for kitchen, kettles' croon,
  kith and kin expected soon.

S for sizzles, sights, and sounds,
  and something special that abounds.

That spells THANKS—for joy in living
and a jolly good Thanksgiving.

Aileen Fisher

INDEX